YOU can help look, too!

First they looked in the cleaning closet.
What do you think they found?
"My long-lost umbrella," cried Mixed Up Max.

"Oh my," thought Gertie Goose.
"That's a MOP!"

They looked in the kitchen cabinet.
What do you think they found?
"My long-lost tennis racket,"
cried Mixed Up Max.

"Dear me," thought Gertie Goose.
"It's a FRYING PAN!"

They looked in the refrigerator.
What did they find?
"My long-lost light bulbs," cried Mixed Up Max.

"Oh no," thought Gertie Goose.
"It's a carton of EGGS!"

They looked in the toy chest.
What did they find?
"My long-lost beach ball,"
cried Mixed Up Max.

"How silly," thought Gertie Goose.
"That's a GLOBE!"

They looked in the dresser drawer.
What did they find?
"My favorite tie," cried Mixed Up Max.

"Good gracious," thought Gertie Goose.
"It's only a SOCK!"

They looked behind the shower curtain.
What did they see?
"My long-lost candy bar," cried Mixed Up Max.

"Oh dear," thought Gertie Goose.
"That's a bar of SOAP!"

They looked in the desk.
What did they see?
"My long-lost screwdriver," cried Mixed Up Max.

"Oh no," thought Gertie Goose.
"It's a PENCIL!"

They looked in the hall closet.
What did they find?
"My long-lost cowboy hat," cried Mixed Up Max.

"Dear me," thought Gertie Goose.
"He's found a LAMPSHADE!"

They looked in the outdoor workshed.
What did they find?
"My long-lost golf club," cried Mixed Up Max.

"For goodness sakes," said Gertie Goose,
"that's a garden HOE! I do hope we find
your glasses SOON!"